KATHLEEN STEVENS

When the Leaves Start to Fall

....

This is a thought-provoking book, which tells how futile war really is, in the eyes of all mankind.

authorHOUSE®

AuthorHouse™
1663 Liberty Drive
Bloomington, IN 47403
www.authorhouse.com
Phone: 1-800-839-8640

Published by AuthorHouse   04/30/2013

ISBN: 978-1-4817-8576-1 (sc)
ISBN: 978-1-4817-8577-8 (e)

Dedicated to the memory of my Uncle Charles, who survived being captured by the Japanese in Burma during World War Two, and to whom I owe a debt of gratitude for his contribution towards some of the detail in the story.

Also to my children, Tony, Juliet, Paula and Janine, for their support and inspiration, and my grandchildren, Angus, Dominic, Finley and Ruby, that they may never witness the futility of War, thereby growing up with happiness, fulfilment and wisdom.

My name is Hannah Mary Smith, and as I am now nearly 90 years of age, I have to live the rest of my days in a Nursing Home. There is plenty of time for reminiscing. At this moment in time, I am gazing out of my window over a panorama of beautiful, colourful autumnal trees in rural New England. I want to relate my story to the world . . . . a story of passion . . . . of wartime survival . . . . and of a love that overcame the hardship and struggle of insurmountable odds, to endure throughout eternity. It begins on a balmy day in late summer of 1943 . . . . when the leaves start to fall . . . .

CONTENTS

CHAPTER ONE

HOME OF CHRISTIAN PITSLEY, AMBER, NEW ENGLAND, 1943

Hannah's tale begins back in her student days at College, with her childhood sweetheart, both learning to be teachers, and loving their life in Amber. His name is Christian Pitsley, also aged nineteen, and as they have known each other since schooldays, both families presume them to get married one day, raise a family, and live in the same small town. Their families live close together in a tree-lined avenue. Each Fall, the whole area is transformed from green, through shades of yellow, brown, and gold, culminating in a beautiful amber colour. It is this last shade that gives their town it's name. Little are they both to realise, at this point in time, the significance of these trees!!

At home, on one particular day, Christian notices an Article in the local Newspaper, about young men needed to volunteer to fight in the Second World War in the Far East. Up until recently, he had not given the War a thought, as it was being fought initially in Europe, and as his family was not connected in any way with anything Military, it has never been a subject they'd talked about much. Until now . . . . for some reason, the Article sparked something in Christian's mind, which he can't put a name to. He becomes curious to find out what type of man could possibly want to put his life on the line, yet in some way, he cannot put the paper down without some feeling of obligation. The Americans have heard that their country is involved in the War, and it is now a major subject of conversation in every household.

Christian can think of nothing else, and wants to read every Newspaper to see what type of man would be suitable for such a massive conflict. He thinks long and hard about whether to join the Military, or to carry on with his studies to become a Teacher. He decides to leave the subject until visiting Hannah in the evening, and to discuss it with her, which is only fair, he thinks. He secretly has an idea she will not want him to go at all, but hopes at least they can talk about it together.

In the early evening, Christian visits Hannah at her home, and as soon as she sets eyes on him, she knows something is bothering him. After he tells her about the Article, and his feelings when he had read it, he lets her know how important it will be to him to participate in the War effort. She surprises him by saying she'd be happy for him to go to join the Military. She also says she would never stand in the way of anything he wants to accomplish., even if it meant him risking his life in the conflict. Christian is silent for a minute, then answers in a faltering and hesitant way,

"Thank you for respecting my decision. Many of my friends are volunteering too, and it is important for me to feel that I'm doing my share in fighting for my country. Training starts after I sign up at the Office of the Military. After a few months, I should be ready to travel to the Far East to join the fighting. Let's have supper, and think about what this means to us as a couple. Absence makes the heart grow fonder is an old saying, which I believe to be true!"

The two of them sit at the kitchen table, munching on toast, and while Christian appears to be able to eat normally, Hannah finds the food gets stuck in her throat. Maybe this is an omen, thinks Hannah, of what is to come, and shudders at the thought!! A fleeting negative thought flashes through her mind, and she quickly dismisses it, at the same time wondering if there could be some significance in it!

Christian seems to read her mind, sensing the negative feeling, but says lovingly, "Goodnight, my darling, I'll see you tomorrow at College, then after classes are over for the day, I'll visit the Military Office for information."

At 4pm the next day, Christian gets on a bus to the nearby town, and walks to the Office as he'd planned. At the desk is a uniformed Officer who produces papers for him to sign. After this is over, the latter commences a brief list of attributes a soldier must possess before he can be considered. As well as the obvious things like health, fitness, good eyesight, and hearing, the man must also be prepared to be away fighting until the end of the War, or until injury puts him out of action, whichever is the soonest. Next on the list, is an appointment in the next building with a Doctor, who checks his lungs with his stethoscope, his heart, and finally, he has a eyesight test, all of which Christian passed successfully.

The training is spread over a few months, he's told, with the ability to use weapons successfully of the utmost importance. With feelings of anticipation coupled with anxiety and apprehension, Christian signs up without hesitation. He thinks to himself, as he departs the Office, that the training will give him an idea of what lies ahead, with regard to combat, but how can one ever be trained into dealing with death on a daily basis. Little does he know though, that the months of training could never ever prepare him for what is to come on the other side of the world!!

He has been accepted due to his young age, health and fitness. He is to commence the necessary training within a week, at the Camp outside the nearby town. For approximately five to six months, he is to learn jungle warfare, along with armaments training, while today, he has to decide to tell Hannah all about how his plan is progressing. He wants to meet her the next day after lessons are over, for an update.

In the cosy College coffee bar, the two sit opposite each other, gazing into each other's eyes, whereupon Christian starts the difficult part of the conversation, stating he will be fighting in Burma, with an unknown length of time the main issue. After a few minutes of digesting the information, Hannah speaks, quietly and lovingly.

"I would never stop you from doing something you want to do, so you have my blessing. How about we marry on your return, as that will give us both something to focus on, to look forward to?"

Christian cannot stop tears flowing down his cheeks now, as he tries to speak, but the words get stuck in his throat. "I will hold you to that. Now I must go home and get my belongings ready for the Camp, and catch up with you at College tomorrow, as I have to write and give in my temporary resignation."

If he had had the remotest idea of what is going to ensue when he's in the Far East, Christian might just have felt some conscience when uttering those words!!

Next morning, he wakes with renewed optimism. He starts the day by gathering together clothing, and documents he'll need for the Training Camp. He feels excited about the prospect of being in a disciplined environment and of making new friends in the Military, all with the same purpose, fighting for their country. Before anything else, he must write the letter to College and take it into the office on the way to his last class. This he does so, feeling positive now about his chosen destiny

After delivering the letter, and taking part in his final classes, Christian meets Hannah, and they walk hand in hand home down the colourful avenue, gazing up at the trees and silently wondering what life has in store for them now that everything has changed. He tells Hannah that they only have about three days together before Training Camp, and decide to make the most of it.

"How about we have a leaving party at my house tomorrow night, Hannah/?" Christian asks. "You can invite your parents and we could have a barbeque and a drink together, then tell them that we intend to marry on my return, and let them all know about my future plans in the Far East."

They kiss goodbye, and Hannah walks the rest of the way home, thinking what a good idea to have a party. As soon as she arrives home, she mentions it to her mom, who also thinks it a great idea. In bed that night, Hannah finds it hard to sleep, with things going round and round in her head. She's trying to be brave and look on the positive side. At the same time, she has an uneasy feeling that she can't put into words. After a fitful night's sleep, she leaves for College in the morning, sees Christian momentarily in the corridor, then starts the day's classes, but knowing full well that she will not possibly be able to concentrate on them.

At 6pm that evening, Hannah and her parents arrive at Christian's home and everyone enjoys the barbeque, despite the weather turning nasty as soon as the food is ready. They finish off with drinks in the house, while Christian relates to everyone his Training schedule, the posting to Burma, and lastly their intention to marry when he returns after the War.

As he is speaking, Hannah happens to look out of the kitchen window and sees leaves suddenly falling in a batch, all on their own, yet nowhere else have any leaves fallen so far this Fall. She thinks how weird, but brushes it off as without explanation.

After saying their goodnights, the family departs for home, and as Hannah walks down the path, she is aware of a neat pile of brown leaves at the bottom, almost as if someone has deposited them in one spot., and they're all brown, instead of a mixture of colours, as is usually the case. They are all dead leaves, she thinks to herself. How strange. She is even more freaked out by this sight, but again, distracts herself with other things. No sooner do they get in their car, than they're arriving home, and Hannah jumps gladly into bed, as if sleep could block out any undesirable thoughts.

CHAPTER TWO

TRAINING TIME

Two days later, Christian is rushing down the road to the local bus stop, where he catches the bus to the Training Camp, clutching a large rucksack and his documents. On arrival at the Camp, he is shown to his bunk, whereupon he commences to unpack and get to know his fellow roommates. He is pleased to know that they are every bit as nervous as he is. During the next few days, he embarks on an intense physical fitness course, the like of which he'd never done before. The Lieutenant who is responsible for giving them advice and enthusiasm, has the loudest voice Christian has ever heard, and it's hard not to obey his every word !!

As the days go by, he finds the training a little easier as he adapts to the requirements. He believes he will master the weaponry part of the training easier than the physical part, as he is used to going to a Firing Range with his father since being young teenager. Each day starts with a 6am wake-up call, followed by two hours of intense exercise before breakfast. The Officer in charge of training the men leaves nothing undone, nothing to the imagination, with everything explained thoroughly in detail. Christian can't help thinking that he had the loudest voice he'd ever heard!!

Day in, day out, the training is the same. Christian is beginning to feel fitter, stronger and more focused than ever. He makes friends with the other men, and is popular with everyone. As the end of the Course draws near, each of the men are beginning to feel that this is only the start, as something much bigger and more meaningful and scary is around the corner, that is, fighting in a World War!!

With the advent of aviation, the ability to get to the other side of the world is now possible in a much shorter time than previously, when all trips were taken by ship. However, the conflict that Christian's Platoon will be involved in, doesn't include having to drop bombs from aircraft, or any other type of airborne combat. They will be fighting purely on the ground, in the jungle, and even face to face!!

On leaving day, Christian gathers his signed documents together and walks off after shaking hands with the Lieutenant, who wishes him luck, adding that he will certainly need it. Christian liked to think of fighting as a new experience, a project, from which he will come away a stronger, wiser man. In fact, he comes away a changed man, from which there is no recovery! At this point in time, this is the last thing on his mind.

He climbs onto the bus to Amber and as he sits in the seat gazing at the scenery flashing by, he has a sudden bolt of anxiety flashing through his mind, but tries to brush it off and focus instead on the prospect of seeing Hannah this evening, and telling her what the last day at Camp was like. When he arrives at her parents' house, she is running down the path to meet him, and as she does so, Christian has a momentary rush of negativity cross his mind, like a lightening bolt! It becomes a frequent phenomenon which will plague him for the rest of his time in Burma! The sight of her outstretched arms is imprinted on his brain, similar to being branded.

After a passionate embrace, the two enter the house, mouths watering at the sight and smell of her Mom's cooking. In Christian's mind, he can't help thinking this is akin to a "last supper!" He tells both parents that he has to finish the term at College first, as he has been informed by the Principal that to gain his qualification at the end, he must take final exams, despite having had a temporary break for Military Training. This is important to Christian and won't take long. The War in the Far East is calling him and he now cannot wait to get those Exams out of the way and get fighting. He tells them all it will soon be time to leave Amber, and will let them know the date, so they can see him off at the train station. With this sorted, they eat supper, mostly in silence, as for some reason, no-one can think of anything positive to say. What does one say to a man who is leaving to go to War, with a high probability he won't be coming back??

Christian kisses Hannah goodnight, stating he must go home to tell his own parents his news, and runs off down the road. At home, both his parents are still up, so he fills them in on the plan and what lies ahead for him in Burma. Obviously they are apprehensive to say the least, as Christian is their only son, but on seeing how brave and positive he's trying to be, they take pride in his efforts and his accomplishments at the Camp, and this overrides their sense of anxiety. They both wish him good luck and go to bed with heavy hearts. Christian sits by the fire for a few moments, deep in thought, before retiring for the night . . . . a night which turns out to be an eventful one!

He's hardly put his head on the pillow before he's dreaming. There is a long road stretching ahead and Hannah is at the end of it, walking slowly towards him with outstretched arms. However, the more he walks towards her, the further away she appears to be, till eventually, she disappears altogether in a fog. As Christian stops in his tracks, leaves start falling from the trees above him, not just a few like in the Fall, but tons of them all at once, covering him from head to foot. He finds it hard to breathe as he lies in the road, and struggles to push a way out, fighting for breath, till suddenly, he wakes up, sweating and fighting to get out of his bed covers! He is panicstricken at the feeling of being smothered, and sits up in bed, wondering what does the dream mean. It must have some significance, he thinks, and even if it doesn't, what is it trying to tell him? With these thoughts going round in his head, he finally falls into a disturbed sleep.

Next day, Christian departs for College to revise for Exams, and to meet Hannah at the end of the day, for a catch-up, wanting to forget about the previous night's dream and fill his thoughts with positive stuff. As he walks down the road, he can't help looking up at the trees above, and wondering if at any minute they may shed their leaves right there and then!

The day is spent in the library with revision taking priority, culminating with a meeting with Hannah, and leisurely walk home. Christian is fully aware that on the way down the road, he is purposely avoiding walking underneath any trees, which Hannah has noticed but doesn't comment. There are more important things on her mind. She is formulating an idea for herself, as the end of summer term is approaching, with a long vacation ahead. As she is so much in love with Christian, she believes it may be possible for her to go to Burma as a temporary teacher. At College, she has often seen positions available abroad for teaching assignments for students with a yearning to experience something new. Also, she feels the separation from Christian may be less difficult if she were at least in the same country. At the moment though, she decides to tell no-one of this idea, till she knows it is possible.

After a few weeks accomplishing revising and exams, Christian's time is getting close to depart the country. He is increasingly nervous at the prospect, the nearer the date becomes!

He calls it "D Day", with reference to the departure. And before long it is actually here.

CHAPTER THREE

THE DEPARTURE

There is a sombre mood in the Pitsley family home this day, which they all cover up by busying themselves with last-minute arrangements. In Hannah's home, a similar mood is prevalent. It's the first time in Mom and Pop Pitsley's life, that they've had to say goodbye to an offspring going to War.

When it's time for Christian and his family to leave for the train station, there are feelings of trepidation all round, and the short drive is taken in complete silence. At one point on the journey, he has a momentary loss of control, when he realises the possibility exists that he may have to kill a man, or many! The thought fills him with dismay, so he dismisses it without further ado. As the car trundles into the car park, they see Hannah and her parents, who are there early, as if every last minute with Christian is special to Hannah, which of course it is.

The families gather on the platform, whereupon he hugs them all and says his goodbyes. Then it's Hannah's turn, to which, in respect for the lovers, the parents then walk away, while Christian takes this opportunity to relates his dream to her. While she wipes away the tears, he explains that what he has to tell her, will give her a positive outlook to hang on to in the long months ahead.

"Hannah, look around you at the trees starting to shed their leaves. Well, I know I'll come home by this time next year, as I had a dream during which I am walking up our street towards you, with outstretched arms, greeting you on my arrival home from the War. As I do so, the first leaves fall on my shoulders. That's when I will come back to you, like in my dream." What Christian doesn't tell her, however, is that the dream turned into a nightmare when he found himself struggling to survive! He tries not to show Hannah that he is in any way anxious, and banishes these thoughts from his mind.

Now it's Hannah's turn to reply, "I will always love you, forever. When the leaves start to fall, I will look out for you, in our street. Goodbye, my darling Christian, and please write to me and let me know your location, so I may send letters back to you. Thanks for telling me about your dream. It does help to know there is a time-line on the length of your posting, as you're so far from home. Please, don't ever stop loving me, no matter what."

As Christian boards the train, he parents have one last wave and walk off, trying not to let him see their tearful faces. He waves to Hannah before the slowly receding platform disappears completely from view. When there is nothing left to see other than the countryside, Christian wipes away his tears and focuses on his immediate future. The train trip is short, and soon the airport buildings are visible on the horizon, instantly reminding him of the reality of his mission!

Although Christian had taken to the training well, he is now filled with apprehension concerning the up-and-coming conflict. Until now, the War had appeared to be something that belonged to others in distant lands, and he had felt safe in the small town of Amber, far from fighting of any type. Now, the reality is striking home, and he feels an urge to take the next train back home! Shrugging off these thoughts, he gets off the train, and hurries to the Departure Point for the Military Personnel. He notices other men in uniform similar to his, all with heavy rucksacks, and looking equally as nervous. They are to board the special plane reserved for Personnel, standing on the runway like a bird of prey, with a massive wingspan, waiting to take off!!

Christian queues, documents held tightly in his sweaty palms, and very soon, they are told to board the flight. It will take them approximately twenty-four hours to get to Bangkok, with many scheduled stops for refuelling. Lots of time to collect thoughts and make plans, thinks Christian to himself! All he wants to do is sleep, to block out any negative thoughts that may creep into his head, but as soon as he nods off, the same dream comes back to him, in exactly the same way as the one he had the previous night. When he gets to the part where he is struggling to breathe, he wakes up, and is confronted by a Military Lieutenant, asking him is he is alright! He decides it's necessary to stay awake for the rest of the flight, and reads brochures given to each man when they had left the Training Camp. As the plane eventually descends into Bangkok, Christian turns his thoughts to Hannah and her sad face looking up at him, and of his Mom, trying so hard to be brave!

The announcement from the Pilot that they are about to land, prompts him to steer his thoughts towards the next few days, of acclimatising to a different culture, climate and atmosphere, and of remembering exactly what they have come to the other side of the world to do! This is not a tourist flight, and the trip is not a holiday! The Platoon are told to go straight to waiting jeeps after disembarking from the aircraft, which will take them to their Camps. Well, thinks Christian, as he takes his first step onto foreign soil, this really is it!!

The jeeps speed out of the confines of the airport, along muddy roads, full of locals on small motorbikes and pushbikes, past villages with people carrying produce on their backs that look larger than they are, and pass many similar jeeps going in the opposite direction. Christian thinks they may be carrying injured soldiers back to civilization, or Hospitals, a sobering thought which makes him physically shiver.

In an hour, the Platoon arrives at the Camp, and the men are asked to muster in a group while being told the details of their posting, and what is expected of them in the next few days. At this meeting, they are able to ask questions, and are shown where each of their bunks are located in large canvas tents. With the whole Platoon feeling exhausted after the flight, they are allowed to retire early for their first night. Christian can't help noticing a strange aroma in the hot, humid air, but cannot put a name to what it reminds him of. Somehow, it remained something he was destined never to get used to!

CHAPTER FOUR

CAMP IN THE JUNGLE

Meanwhile, back in Amber, and trying hard to concentrate on something other than Christian's whereabouts, Hannah is back at College. For some reason, she cannot get out of her mind the dream that Christian told her about. It has left her feeling decidedly weird, uneasy, like the possibility of impending doom is just round the corner. Strange, she has just fast-forwarded the following year in her mind, but is not aware of it!

She is carrying on with her studies, and cannot wait to hear from Christian, wondering how he is feeling and whether he's adapted to the strange country yet. The idea she had already thought of, she finds she can accomplish quite soon, as her exams are near now. She has looked at the Notice Boards at Volunteer Placements in remote areas around the world. Its for anyone with suitable qualifications and a couple of month's vacation to spare. She thinks by applying for one of these posts, she will be near to Christian, or so she believes. There could even be a possibility that he could visit her there during his leave. She speaks to her Mom about it.

"Mom, I've a brilliant idea. When my exams are over, which is quite soon, I'm going to apply for a temporary teaching post in Burma, to be close to where Christian is fighting, and maybe he could then visit me during his time off. As soon as I hear from him with his location, I'll write and tell him of my idea."

Hannah's Mom is not very impressed with the plan, but has to let her make up her own mind, while wanting her to do her research properly first, to find the best places, locations, and environment, before she makes any further plans. The same evening, Hannah finds an atlas, and makes notes of place names. Tomorrow, she plans to get details of schools in and around Bangkok.

Next morning, in break from class, she sees two suitable posts for Teaching Assistants, which are in the outskirts of Bangkok, and commences to write application letters to both. She then catches up with preparation for exams. She decides there and then that the following week will be the start of the next phase of her plan, as that is when the exams will be over. At this moment in time, she has not the remotest idea of the twist of fate awaiting her, and even if she did, she would still carry on with the same plan of action, believing that the love she and Christian share could never change!

Meanwhile, at the Camp in the jungle clearing in Burma, while Christian's Platoon have all been allocated their bunks, they find it difficult to imagine this place could ever feel like home, and are told to meet for a briefing first thing next morning. The Lieutenant in charge of the men's welfare, is named Foley, and is extremely forceful in his mannerisms, with a voice like thunder! He orders the men to sort out their belongings, and at the briefing, he will let them know the plan of action for the conflict. In this large tent, Christian is sharing with two others. One is named Stuart, and the other, a giant of a man, is named James. (Little does Christian realise, at this point in time, the significance of James' size.)

Christian decides to introduce himself to the others. They all three speak cautiously, one at a time, telling a little about where they come from, and how they feel about their part in the War. Evidently, both Stuart and James had left wife and children behind in America, and the anguish they felt is plain to see. Christian's plight at leaving a girlfriend only, pales into insignificance when he knows about the other two's dependents.

After a fitful night's sleep, the three men emerge from the tent to listen to what Lieutenant Foley has to say, while they all admit feeling intimidated by the man.

16

The Lieutenant speaks to the Platoon. "Well everyone, you can see how we will be living, now I aim to tell you how we will be fighting. You will take up your allocated firearms tomorrow first thing, and divide into groups. We fight with rifles, and use grenades. Our enemy, the Japanese, are very clever, and because the jungle is so dense, you never see them. Cutting through the undergrowth is something you will get used to. Our aim is to push the enemy out of the jungle, and eventually drive them towards the border. No-one will complain, as you have all received the necessary training, albeit not in a jungle setting. However, you'll soon get used to the noises, animals and the smell!!

There is a meal distributed to each man, thrown into an aluminium can, consisting of what looks like rice with additives, the contents of which no-one wants to analyze. The men are then free to experience what the jungle has to offer, which is quite frightening to small town people. They are to sort their guns, ammunition, uniform, and get over jetlag, before starting fighting the next day. When the night comes in Burma, it happens all of a sudden, and then the noises start, first a shrill sqeaking, then deeper barking, which resonates throughout the dense jungle. It prevents the men from sleeping properly, so when they wake early the next morning, they feel like they've hardly slept.

At 7am Lieutenant Foley's voice booms out in the hot, still air of the jungle, telling everyone to get up . . . . and get out . . . .! Breakfast is a quick coffee and what appears to be dry biscuits of sorts. Not a lot for a man fighting all day, think the men, but feel they're lucky to be eating at all in some ways! They are then ordered, in a few short words, to follow the Lieutenant into the jungle and do what he says, but to be vigilant at all times. During the previous night, there have been gunshots in the distance, and noises like muffled grenades exploding . . . This proves to the men what they have heard previously about Japanese, that the enemy rarely sleeps, is active night and day, and is not too far away. The Lieutenant sets off into the trees, after having checked each man's weapons and ammunition. He requests they put foliage into their hats as camouflage. The men realize it's their first experience of battle, and that they have to learn tactics from their leader. They tell each other not to be scared, and that they'll look out for each other, and provide cover for whoever gets into trouble, which happens to be quite soon!! The fact that each man is so scared, must be brushed off, as they need to be focused on the conflict to be able to attack and defend themselves.

As they advance through the trees, every snap of a twig, every noise from a tree overhead and the men jump, trembling. They experience animal noises, birds sounds, and the sight of giant insects the like of which they've never seen before! On hearing sounds of gunfire in the distance, they duck behind foliage. Christian thinks to himself, however does one get used to this fear, the constant threat to one's life, the unexpected?

As each hour passes, the Platoon gets more used to holding and firing their weapons. This particular day, the enemy appear to have set up loudspeakers in the jungle, and the men cannot help thinking how uncanny to hear their voice, but not see them!! By twilight, they return to Camp exhausted, to be briefed about the tasks for the next day, and how much progress has been made today through the jungle.

As the three friends sit down to eat the meagre rations of their evening meal, Christian asks the other two if they know how to get a letter to home, from the jungle. A difficult enough request, he thinks, but there has to be a way! James tells him the he heard the Lieutenant tell someone about the procedure. Evidently there's a collection and delivery service first thing in the morning, once a week. Someone will shout out in Camp that the mail van is here, which doubles up as an arms supply, along with some food rations.

Christian hurriedly eats his supper, as it consists of something he'd rather not think about, and settles down in the tent to write the letter to Hannah. It goes something like this . . . .

Camp in Burma jungle. Day two.
Dearest Hannah,

Well, our Platoon has arrived at the Camp after what feels like a long and tiring journey. It's unbearably hot and humid, and it's hard to fight in these conditions. I'm sure we'll get used to it though. I'll write again to let you know how things proceed, but at the moment, there's nothing much to report as we've only started combat in the last two days. The enemy is clever in that we never see them, but we can hear them.

They're not far away, and fire shots day and night, throw grenades, and there are what sounds like small explosions every so often. We are all so scared, but dare not show it.

At night, it's hard to sleep, because of the noises made by the jungle inhabitants! My love for you grows by the day, my darling Hannah. Thinking of you and can't wait till I receive your letter. Remember . . . . till the leaves start to fall . . . .

From your loving Christian.xxxxxxxx

The men are now sleeping, or trying to, when the jungle noises start, always about the same time every night. Luckily, they're so fatigued that it will take more than animal noises to keep them awake tonight!

At 7am next morning, sure enough, a shout is heard that the mail van is on it's way. There is a mail delivery and collection, before breakfast, and Christian is thankful to see his letter depart in the dirty canvas bag. However, as he walks back to his tent, he's aware that his head is throbbing violently, and grabs it with both hands. James looks at him in a concerned way, realizing it may be serious. He tells Christian to go to the Lieutenant and let him know, as he couldn't possibly join the Platoon for their mission today, not like that! He mentions he's heard of illnesses that are picked up easily in a jungle. Most produce high fevers, which is dangerous, he admits.

Christian immediately visits the Lietenant's tent, and tells him he's ill, of which the latter can see for himself the profuse sweating. He is told to retire to his bunk and the Camp Doctor will visit him soon. The Lietenant gives him some painkillers, and with great difficulty, Christian walks back to his own tent, stooping over with fatigue and weakness. As he does so, there is a loud explosion close to their Camp, upon which everyone drops to the ground instinctively. After a few seconds, there is no other explosion, and the Platoon gradually get up and grab their own weapons. This has been the first experience for the men of such a close shave, a quick reminder that the enemy is now not far away. The rest of the men start out on the daily march, following Lieutenant Foley, and disappearing into the jungle in express time, while Christian waits for the Doctor, with an ever-increasing fever.

An hour later, the Doctor visits Christian and diagnoses Malaria, caught from a mosquito bite, he informs the gravely ill man. He gives Christian drugs to fight the disease, agreeing to visit him again in 24 hours, when there should be a response to the drug. Christian finds it hard to rest, and tosses and turns with an unbearably high fever.

He is delirious when his two comrades return in the evening, and they tell him that he's constantly calling for Hannah, his girlfriend, They are both concerned for Christian as he keeps them all awake that night. At 7am next morning, the Doctor again visits, and immediately phones for a jeep to transport him to the Field Hospital. Within ten minutes, Christian is on a stretcher arriving at the Hospital, barely conscious.

A nurse deals with Christian's primary needs, as she has seen many a Malaria victim before. She is a Burmese named Malay, and speaks very good English. She mops his brow with cold water, trying to lower the fever, while attempting to administer sips of liquid and the drug. He hovers between life and death for the next day, with Malay hardly leaving his side, apart from when yet another wounded soldier arrives on a stretcher. Each time, she then returns to Christian's side and continues with the brow mopping, all through the night. The next morning, Christian opens his eyes for the first time and calls for Hannah, whereupon Nurse Malay rushes to his side. He stares at her in disbelief, thinking he must have died and gone to heaven, such a lovely sight is she to behold!! Nurse Malay fetches him some broth to give him strength to get over the disease, and tells him the fever has broken and he's on the mend. She also tells him he's been calling for someone called Hannah all night.

Well, that's no surprise then, thinks Christian, as Hannah has been on his mind all the time. However, just for a minute, with this vision of beauty now standing beside him, he has somehow forgotten about his girlfriend for an instant, which worries him just a little bit.!

Christian manages a few words, although each one is an effort. "You speak good English, and thank you for caring for me so professionally. Hannah is my girlfriend back in America, and we're very much in love. I miss her so much. I guess you're used to caring for soldiers though, as it's your job, like mine is fighting in this godforsaken War."

Christian stares at the big, brown eyes looking down at him, and feels like he's falling into their depth. Is he having another of those dreams, he thinks to himself, or is this vision standing here, a real live human being. He wants to express something to her, some words with meaning, to tell her how he's feeling. He can't help comparing her to an angel! After what seems an eternity, Christian speaks very quietly, yet it feels like he's listening to someone else saying the words!

"I hope to return to my girlfriend in America when the War if over, and marry her," he says, yet he sounds unconvincing in his pronounciation of the words, like as if he's trying to tell himself that this is what he should be doing!

There is an awkward silence, then Malay speaks, "I prayed for you last night, that you'd live, and my prayers are answered. I will go now and catch up with other wounded soldiers. I'll come back to you this evening with more broth. Meantime, try and get some rest." At this point, Malay senses there is something special about this stranger, this wounded soldier who needs her, but at the same time, she tries to keep herself in check, remembering to keep everything on a professional level, as Nurses are taught.

Christian lies in his bed, feeling a surge of gratitude for this Nurse, this compassionate stranger, whom he feels has saved his life. He thinks how lovely she is, and how he's looking forward to seeing her again in the evening. He drifts off to sleep, but this time, it is Malay he's thinking about, and not Hannah!

Each day for a week, Christian continues to recover, becoming stronger and more able to walk, with the help of Malay's arms round his shoulders. He quietly wonders if she feels any attraction towards him, or is the affectionate arm round his shoulder just part of a Nurse's job. As they walk around the outside of the Hospital, Christian asks her about her life in Burma, before the War came and shattered everything they held dear.

Each day as he's getting stronger, Christian finds he's thinking more about Nurse Malay, than Hannah. He's confused about his feelings. As he leaves the Hospital, he tells Malay that he will return to visit her when he has his next leave, or when the War is over, whichever happens the soonest. He's then transported back to Camp in the same jeep, glad to be meeting up with his close comrades again, but about two stones lighter! The three friends chat together in their tent and James and Stuart fill him in on what has been happening since he left. Evidently, the Japanese have been attacking at night, and two of their Platoon have been severely injured. Christian is horrified to hear this, but has to get used to it, as it gets worse, he thinks to himself. The fact that the enemy are getting cleverer and bolder, is not good news for the Americans.

Deep in the jungle the following morning, the Platoon are busy dodging the enemy, and lying in the undergrowth, waiting for a chance to move forward with their mission to drive the latter out of the area. The day has begun with heavy bombardment of grenades, and progress through the jungle is slow. Another of their group is injured by shrapnel and taken away to Hospital, while Christian is becoming more adept at firing weapons and being part of increasingly heavy combat. Although the men have not sighted the Japanese, they seem to be close in proximity, as their voices can be heard when there is a brief interlude between blasts. This makes the hair on the back of Christian's neck stand on end!!

As they make their way back to Camp for the night, James tells him they'll be moving North to a new location very soon, as they had orders while Christian was in Hospital. This will happen as soon as the enemy are chased out of this part of the jungle, which means they will have retreated. This is good news for Christian, who has really disliked this dense jungle area. After having eaten supper in the dining tent, the three sit in their accommodation, discussing the week's progress, and how they're only now getting used to what is expected of them. None of them has come from a Military background.

Tonight, Christian wants to write to Hannah, telling her of the new posting, but for some reason, being apart from her doesn't bother him as much as it did. Ever since leaving the Hospital, he's thought of nothing but the beautiful Nurse Malay, and her compassionate and caring nature. It is while he is relating to his friends about her, that Christian realizes it's probably gratitude, mixed with missing his girlfriend back home, that has made him turn his feelings away from Hannah, and towards another woman.

At the same time, he knows he's fallen in love with Nurse Malay, and wonders if it's possible to be in love with two people at once! The delerium of his illness had contributed to his confusion in those feelings, and towards whom his love is directed, he thinks. Maybe now is the time to tell Hannah what has happened, to let her know, so he will feel less guilty. He cannot have guilt on his mind when fighting for his life! So he starts writing to her.

"Dear Hannah,

You haven't heard from me for a while, as I've been in Hospital recovering from Malaria, but now am back fighting again in the jungle. However, when I was in Hospital, I developed feelings for my Nurse which I tried to resist, without success. I am so sorry to have to tell you this, as I didn't want anything ever to happen to us. You know how it's only you I've ever loved. This new love happened out of the blue, totally unexpected, and knocked me off my feet.

Soon, we are marching North by about 100 miles and I won't be able to write and send letters. I owe it to you to continue writing to let you know how and where I am, so you can get a reply letter to me. I anticipate you'll want to give your opinion on my news. At present, everything is new and confusing, and I don't even know what's going to happen next. We exist from day to day. When the War is over, I'll make a decision. The Nurse is Burmese, and if our feelings are true, real, and lasting, I will want to stay in this country. I can't believe I'm telling you all this, but out of respect for the length of time we've known each other, you deserve to be told if anything has changed between us.

I cannot now write loving words to you in letters and really mean it wholeheartedly, so I'll keep them friendly and to the point. It seems when I was feverish in Hospital, I called your name. This fact adds to my confusion, as my inner self wanted you, even though the Nurse was there!! I'll sign off now and hope after the initial shock, you can find it in your heart to forgive me. It's not every day that one is at War in the middle of a relationship. Maybe when I return, or if I return, we can be friends. I still love and respect you as a person. Take care of yourself. Please let me know how you are, and what happens with your studies. I do wish you luck. I hope in some way, I may find a way to mail this letter to you one day soon.

Your soul mate,
Christian.

CHAPTER FIVE

HANNAH ARRIVES IN BURMA

Meanwhile, at Hannah's home in Amber, things are happening at a rate of knots!! After she's given in her temporary Notice at College, she's had a reply from one of the two Schools she applied to for a teaching Post. Being excited about this, has given her adrenaline to spur on her plans to leave the country, which in itself is a huge achievement for a young girl, with the advent of air travel. This week, she's sorted her travel Documents, has her flight to Bangkok booked, picked up her qualification papers from College, and made preparations for acclimatising to the new country. She's really done her homework properly, as has poured over maps of the terrain, read about the climate and the people, and found out what days and hours she's expected to work.

This type of overseas temporary work is also quite a new thing, as mostly, in the past, people who took posts abroad, would have taken a ship to their destination, making a much longer voyage time. Most of these posts were for Nanny-type positions, with Teaching Assistants being a relatively new job.

Luckily, Hannah has found out from maps that there is a train station not far from the school where she'll be living. She's apprehensive about leaving home for the first time, but as she knows Christian is in the same country, it's given her added impetus to keep pursuing her mission. Most importantly,

Hannah has always loved children, and the thought of being able to enhance their learning experience, makes her very happy.

So far, she's received only one letter from Christian, to tell her he's arrived in Burma and is ok. She wants to write to him now, letting him know the address of the school where she'll be working, because at this point in time, he has no idea she plans to come to Burma at all. Also, she hasn't received his second letter yet, telling her of his new love, and that they're moving to a different location. Hannah today tells her Mom all about the school on the outskirts of Bangkok, and how excited she is at the prospect of seeing her beloved Christian again. She knows nothing of the shocking letter en route to America, at this moment.

Another three days of preparing, and the day of departure is here. Hannah's parents are waiting in the car when the postman puts a letter in their box at the end of the drive. As they go past it, Hannah requests her Pop to stop, just in case it's a letter from Christian. Sure enough, it's his second letter, and Hannah decides to read it on the plane, as it will give her something to do on the twenty-four hour flight! Maybe something inside her tells her it's bad news, and not to open it yet, not wanting anything to mar her plans, and stop her leaving.

It's not far to the Airport, and Hannah is strangely silent. Her parents can't help but notice it, and put it down to last-minute nerves. They also feel apprehensive that their only daughter is going to the other side of the world. At the Departure Point, they hug each other, with Hannah promising to write as soon as she arrives at the school. As she goes through the point in the Airport building where family can go no further, she waves to her Mom and Pop, and carries on out onto the tarmac. She has one last wave for her parents, and tearfully moves towards the aircraft, hoping against hope that she's doing the right thing.

As Hannah sits in her seat, she suddenly has a strange thought. What if Christian has no leave from fighting, what if he's been killed in action and she hasn't been informed yet, what if he's not in the location he told her about in his letter?? The "what-if's" keep coming! So now is the time to open the letter, she decides, and stop the "what-if's" once and for all. They're probably not real anyway, she thinks.

As she opens the envelope, her face crinkles up, and tears flow down her rosy cheeks, while her heart misses a beat. She tries to stop her hands shaking as she carries on reading down the page, and the writing is blurred as she reads on through the tears. She keeps thinking there must be some mistake, that she will receive another letter saying this has been a flash in the pan, and he's sorry . . . . but, oh no, she realizes, there won't be another letter as he doesn't know she's going to be in Burma now. Hopefully she can send him a letter containing her address, if it will get to him before the Platoon leaves to go North.

She has a determination to carry on with her plans, and to replace devastation with optimism, that things will alter, and that Christian will have a change of heart. She truly believes this has only happened because he's away from her, and their close loving relationship. If she and Christian can meet up in Burma and talk things over, she is sure he will change his mind on seeing her again, and re-kindle their love for one another.

Hannah decides to spend the rest of the flight making plans on what to do in Burma, where it will be easier to find out where American soldiers are located, by searching local Newspapers, and office notice boards for travellers from abroad. She tears up the letter from Christian, as if by doing so, the contents are now forgotten, and didn't really happen anyway. The ripped paper is put into the trash bag attached to the back of the seat, and she proceeds with her mission, oblivious to the other passengers sitting alongside her.

Another 14 hours of flight time, with two more scheduled stops to refuel, and Bangkok Airport is within sight. As the plane nears the ground, a maze of bustling streets can be seen, along with colourful rooftops and vehicles of all shapes and sizes! Outside the Arrivals Building, and after having produced her Passport for perusal by the Authorities, Hannah hails a taxi, and the trip out of the city starts.

Hannah has to hang on to the sides of the vehicle, so crazy is the type of driving undertaken there by taxis. She is glad to be at her destination in one piece!! The cultural differences are enormous, she thinks. Outside the school, she takes stock of the surroundings, after paying the driver for the eventful journey from the Airport. The school building looms up out of what appears to be the ruins of another building, probably the older school, Hannah thinks.

After a welcome briefing by two staff of the school, she goes up to her room, and collapses onto the tiny bed, exhausted. Despite being hungry, she falls asleep straight away. Next morning, about 8am, she goes down to the dining room, with doubles up as an office, a sick room, and a library. These are the culture differences she will come across on her travels in Burma, but still it takes some getting used to. There, she meets some of the other staff, who all speak good English, luckily. Breakfast is taken together, with the staff giving her a rundown of the routine at the school, days off, and hours to be worked, etc. These are all things she's already found out, but it helps her to get close to the rest of the staff, who could be useful when she wants information about Christian's Platoon's whereabouts.

Classes start at 9am each day, with weekends off. Hannah has free time in the evenings too, to become acquainted with her surroundings. She feels an affinity with the children straight away, who welcome her with open arms to their school and country. In the downstairs office, Hannah finds a local map, and more detailed one than the map she brought from home. She plans to study this when she has time, to find the location of Christian's last letter postmark.

Each day is the same, with Hannah enjoying teaching more and more. She is well-loved and respected by all, but deep down, she cannot be herself, as each day too she is thinking of her beloved Christian, and wanting the days to pass quickly, so she can start her search.

She buys a local Newspaper and scours it for information regarding the progress of the War, and what is happening to the American soldiers who are in Burma. She sees a photograph of a Platoon, and wants to get a magnifying glass to get a closer look to see if Christian is there, but as yet, there doesn't seem to be a tool of that nature anywhere, even in the office/sick room/ dining room/library!!

The next morning, she has a stroke of luck, as one of the staff has heard that there is a Platoon of American soldiers close by. With this in mind, Hannah starts to feel more positive about the possibility of finding Christian, and resumes lessons with an added spring in her step. She's only signed up for eight weeks, so it won't be long before she'll be free to start her search. In any case, this temporary post will look good on her C.V. for her future, if she even wants to pursue her plans of becoming a Teacher one day, back in America.

CHAPTER SIX

CAPTURED BY THE JAPANESE

Back in the jungle, the day of heavy bombardment ended with six of the Platoon's men wounded, one fatally. This latter has affected the men's morale greatly, as by now they're like brothers. It is a very dark night tonight, and after supper, there is a discussion about the supposed posting North, which seems now to be imminent. Exhausted, the three friends retire for the night, knowing what they're immediate future now holds, a move from here.

While they sleep, a group of Japanese soldiers come upon the Platoon as they're making their way out of the jungle. The men are woken by the shouts of the two at the front of the group, and everyone is startled! The Japanese proceed to take the whole Platoon, including Lieutenant Foley, prisoner at gunpoint, and march them out of their Camp, then through the jungle for what seemed like an eternity. Having hardly had any sleep, the men are disorientated anyway, and this, coupled with fear, turns the march into a complete nightmare!

At dawn, they arrive at a weird-looking place, the like of which they have never seen before, but which is destined to fill them with horror for a long time to come. It is a sight which is embedded in their minds and will ultimately affect them for the rest of their lives. It doesn't take long for the men to realize what this place is, and what is expected of them from now on.

It is a Japanese Prisoner-of-War Camp. This fact is obvious to all, as it has high walls, interspersed with towers. At the top of each is a Japanese soldier holding a rifle, pointing at the men. Although no-one speaks Japanese, the men know this is serious, as the body language is obvious from the Guards. No-one dares to ask anything, for fear they may utter a Japanese word by accident and it could have the wrong meaning. It looks like the Guards would have no hesitation in shooting any of them at the slightest provocation.

The men are herded like cattle into a makeshift building looking like cages joined together by rope. Christian's heart sinks when he realizes this is the end of any prospect of a visit to Malay, of any leave, or of sending or receiving any letters from home. His family, or his girlfriend will never know about his fate, and he has not the remotest idea how long the men will be kept prisoner. A tear runs down his cheek and falls into his pillow, or what improvises as such.

After a fitful night of sweating, shaking, and fearful feelings, the whole Platoon are told to assemble in the compound in the centre of the Camp to be addressed by the Commandant, whose name they cannot pronounce, or would ever want to! Evidently, their job here is to construct roads through the jungle, involving digging the mud, shovelling into heaps, and walking back and forth from the road, to the prison, for nine hours a day, every day. They are to start immediately, making them feel very despondent about their competence and abilities to complete the task. They all worry about what will happen to them if the relentless humidity and heat renders them unable to work after they become fatigued. The whole Platoon has already lost weight in the jungle due to fighting without proper nourishment.

Christian and his friends discuss the fact that in here, they won't ever know how the War is progressing, meaning they won't know either how long they could be held prisoner for. In this situation, the larger your body size, the longer you can last working in the heat. James, being the larger of the three men, and by far the stronger, tries to help Christian, who has not yet recovered fully from Malaria. Each day, when they start work on the roads, and when the Guards are not looking, James takes over from Christian, finishing digging his part of the trench, while the ever-weaker latter hides in the ditch. If James is seen to be helping any of the others, he would be shot, so Christian is well aware of the risks James is taking on his behalf. This feat of comradeship between the men in their Platoon, is something Christian will never ever forget.

Meanwhile, back in Bangkok, Hannah has received no news of Christian's whereabouts as obviously, he doesn't even know she is in Burma living and working. A month passes by at the school, with Hannah enjoying her job, and becoming close to her pupils. One evening, during her free time, she thinks it a good idea to give her parents a telephone call, to see if any letters have arrived at the family home, from Christian, recently. Luckily, there is a phone booth across the road, and her Mom is excited to hear from her that she's doing well at her job. Hannah asks if there are any letters for her, and Mom says one arrived only the previous day. She asks her Mom to read it out loud to her, but it turns out to be just a courtesy note, informing her that he is safe, and the conflict has moved further North, saying at the end that he will let her know the address of the Camp in due course.

Hannah's Mom is puzzled, as she is not aware that Christian knows nothing of Hannah's plans to teach in Burma. She says nothing out of respect for her daughter's privacy, but does have one bit of good news, that the postmark of the letter is "Mantang." At least, Hannah knows he is alive and where the Camp is. That news gives her some adrenaline to move her forward in her search, as she remembers seeing a place of that name on the map back in her room.

To complete her job's requirement, she needs to work another two weeks. In this time, Hannah is researching in the evenings after classes. She's found Mantang, a small town not far from the school. On the morning of leaving day, she bids the staff and children an emotional farewell, and with a heavy heart, makes her way to the local train station. She plans to take the tiny train to Mantang, and to find lodgings for the next couple of days. This will give her chance to make enquiries of locals, about news of any American Soldiers in the vicinity.

She has a few minutes on the overcrowded train, to overhear the conversations of other passengers. What bothers her is the fact that Japanese soldiers are everywhere, and it's heard they take people prisoner and put them into Camps. The poor people then are put to work on construction of roads and bridges in the intense heat of the jungle. Hannah thinks to herself how tragic War is, and cannot find a purpose for the suffering of the human race. As she watches the countryside rush past, she hasn't the remotest idea of the trauma to come to her, in a short time.

A loud whistle announces the train's arrival at Mantang, which instantly wakes Hannah from her daydream. She steps off the train, her heart pounding, almost as if she expects to see Christian standing on the platform waiting for her!! Deep down, she knows this is not possible, after all, he doesn't even know she's here.

She walks down the narrow streets teeming with locals, animals and bicycles. She skirts round unexpected craters in the pavements till she spots what looks like a Tourist Information Office. Inside, there's a notice board with information on transport, lodgings, and public services. She picks out a telephone number of a guest house, and calls it from a phone booth across the road. She then calls a taxi which drops her to the door, driven by a very bemused driver. This is because it's rare to see a blonde female alone, roaming around in Burma.

Inside the Guest House, a strange sight meets her eyes. The is a local male receptionist, all four feet of him, who, according to the sign over the counter, doubles up as a chauffeur, a gardener, a valet, and a Doctor!! Hannah thinks maybe a dentist is included in this list, and shudders at the thought. What a culture shock. The tiny man shows her to her room, which has obviously seen better days. However, Hannah is so thankful to have found accommodation, that she accepts it without further ado.

She asks the receptionist if he's heard of any American soldiers in the area, and his answer shocks her. "Yes, there was a Platoon of soldiers a few miles outside of this town, living in a large Camp, but suddenly, they disappeared. That was a week ago, and the locals are puzzled as to what happened to them. Why do you ask?"

Hannah tells him she's looking for a friend of hers from America, and that her Teaching job is now over here, giving her time to search for him. The tiny man nods his head as if he already knows it must be a lost love of hers, to which Hannah then tells him briefly what has happened recently, to bring her to Burma. She thanks him for his understanding, and gets ready for bed, too anxious and excited to feel hungry. She wants to lie in bed and plan her next move. An Office of the Military, if she can find one, is a good place to start, she thinks, as she slowly drifts off to sleep.

Next morning, she goes into a shop in the centre of the town, and manages to get some information from a local man. He tells her there has been a Camp of American soldiers not far away, but they suddenly disappeared a week ago. He also says that locals will not venture far out of the town, as Japanese soldiers are patrolling the areas of Northern Burma and everyone fears them. Hannah decides it's a good idea to ask a taxi driver to take her around a three mile radius of the town, to which the first one she asks, agrees. The driver does say, though, that he will make a hasty retreat if any Japanese soldiers are spotted.

After twenty minutes driving, Hannah sees a clearing beside the road, which looks like there may have been activity there. She requests that the taxi driver wait for her while she goes to have a search of the area. He agrees to wait, telling her to be extremely vigilant.

As she treads carefully across the clearing, she sees signs that tents have been erected there, as the shape on the dry grass can be depicted.

Just as she turns round to head back to the taxi, there is the sound of crackling twigs. Hannah freezes in her tracks, as there, right in front of her, are a group of Japanese soldiers, holding rifles and pointing them straight at her. Terrified, she holds her arms up in the surrender position, trying not to appear as frightened as she feels. They make a sign for her to move forward, and with a rifle held against her back, they march her through dense trees. After what seems an eternity, the group arrive at a Camp in another clearing. She is blindfolded, much to her annoyance, then one of the soldiers pushes her down onto what feels like a canvas chair, while another tries to find a Japanese who can speak some English.

In a matter of minutes, in which time stands still for Hannah, a loudly-spoken soldier pulls off the blindfold roughly, telling her, via an interpreter, that she is now a Prisoner-of-War of the Japanese, and from now on, she will do as she's told. He points to a large dormitory-type tent, telling her that this will be her home for the near future.

Hannah can't believe she should have this bad luck while searching for Christian. How unfair and scary, she thinks, as she finds an empty bunk. She hasn't heard of women being captured by Japanese soldiers before, thinking it was only men that were put into these Camps. However, she is soon to hear that in this particular country, it has happened, whereas the locals had not heard of women being captured anywhere else in the Far East. Maybe, thinks Hannah, this is another issue of War, man's inhumanity to man . . . . or in her case, man's inhumanity to women!

A quick look around the tent, and she notices hundreds of female prisoners packed in to such a small place, looking as terrified as she felt. There are mostly Burmese women, of different ages, and Hannah feels a sudden surge of loneliness, realizing no-one will be speaking English. With sign language of sorts, she is told by the others, that they have to do manual work eight hours a day, seven days a week. Wondering why these women have been taken prisoner, is what Hannah ponders about all the time she's in the Camp. She daren't ask her captors why she's there, as they look much too frightening as people, to even approach.

She copies the other women as much as she can, and after a restless night's sleep, wakes up with the utmost dread, when realises where she is. There is a sudden shout, and a soldier appears at the doorway to beckon them out, holding the inevitable rifle. They are expected to be ready for work at 7am each morning.

Everyone is to stand to attention in the middle of the compound, for instructions from the Commandant. It appears that anyone straying into an area patrolled by the Japanese, will be captured and detained in a Camp till the end of the War. What a sobering thought for Hannah, when all the while, she wants desperately to find Christian. This cancels all her plans of finding him, and she now feels she's sinking into full-blown despair. He will now never know what has happened to her, till the end of the War, and there is no way of letting him know.

After another five minutes listening to more orders, with a broken-English Interpreter, they all know they are to work in the fields, planting and digging, or, if they're lucky, they get to work inside the Camp, on laundry duties. Anyone who becomes too weak to work, or too ill, or doesn't work properly, will be shot immediately. What is more, work is to start right now, and there is no mention of food, rest, days off, or a finishing time. The horror this produces in the women's minds, is indescribable. Hannah thought, in hindsight, she should have listened to that taxi driver, who tried to tell her how foolish to go into the jungle alone when the Japanese are known to be in the area.

Meanwhile, the day in the fields has started, with the heat and humidity almost unbearable. Hannah can't help thinking how long the women can be expected to work in these conditions, as even on her first day there, one of the women has collapsed. After the latter had been spirited away quickly by two Guards producing a stretcher, she hasn't been seen since. As if this were not enough, by the end of the day, two more older women have fainted and have been half dragged, half carried back to the accommodation by the rest of the group.

Next morning, while Hannah is busy in the fields, one of the Japanese Guards appears to be staring straight at her, making her feel very uncomfortable, but she cannot understand why. It's not as if she can remember doing anything wrong at all. She thinks back now to the previous day, when she became aware of the same Guard staring at her then. On this particular day though, he actually beckons to her to go to him, producing shaking and fear inside the poor girl.

He takes her into the shed-like building used for storing supplies. She thinks he's showing her what job needs to be done there, but instead, to her horror, he beckons for her to remove her clothing. As he's a rifle on his arm, she feels she must obey. Still trembling, she feels physically sick as he touches her all over her body, running his hands up and down her shape. Hannah thinks to herself that this is what indecent assault is, and that at any minute, someone may enter the building without warning, and they would both be shot!

In two minutes, it's all over, and Hannah's eyes are kept tightly shut, as if by doing so, she can tell herself that this is not really happening. Obviously, the Guard has had the same thought, about another Guard entering, as he stops abruptly, indicating to her to put her clothes back on.

It seems that for allowing this indecent assault, Hannah now has privileges. She's singled out for better treatment, finishes working in the fields, and instead, is told to look after the Commandant's rooms, and also to be in charge of laundry duties. Each day, though, while doing these, she dreads a repeat of the assault. Luckily for Hannah, the Guard also sees the futility of risking his own life for this one act, and never asks her again.

Back in her accommodation later that night, she cannot help thinking about War, it's meaning, and the terrible acts it allows one human being to commit against another human being, which in ordinary daily life, one would be punished by law for!

Life at the women's Camp goes on the same every day, with the other women in Hannah's accommodation block wondering why she suddenly left working with them in the fields, and is now inside the Commandant's buildings, with much better working conditions. Hannah never wants them to know the truth of what happened on that terrible day, and from then on, till release from the Camp, no-one else ever knew.

En route back to her accommodation block one day, Hannah can't help but notice a group of buildings that look similar to their Camp, in the distance, with high walls and towers. These towers also had Japanese Guards at the top, with rifles. She wants a better look, and decides to walk round the compound and peer through the fence, without it appearing obvious. What an ironic thing this is, as, little does Hannah know, but she is staring straight at the Camp where the love of her life is being held captive. As half a kilometre separates the two Camps, there is no way either of them could ever know that they are so close to one another!! She will never know she has found her Christian at last, without taking another step in the search.!

CHAPTER SEVEN

THE NEWS IS GOOD

Meanwhile in Camp, the three friends are trying to eat supper, despite being almost too exhausted to pick their spoons up to their mouths. They're having a discussion on how the lack of nourishment is contributing to their demise. Christian admits to the other two, that he doesn't know how long he can keep going, digging and carrying buckets of heavy soil backwards and forwards in the relentless heat, on such frugal rations. James replies with similar despondency, that there has to be a way of finding out what is happening in the outside world. He says he has a thought. If they could listen to their Captor's Wireless which is located in a hut by the gate in the compound, it could give them an idea of how the War is progressing. He thinks if the three of them walk around the perimeter of the compound after supper, and stop to chat beside the hut, they can then listen to the Wireless.

The other two think this is a great idea, and decide that the next day, they can accomplish the plan. Somehow the very thought of it gives them a modicum of positivity in an otherwise negative environment, like one step towards untimate freedom!

So, the next evening, Christian and Stuart start walking slowly around the compound while James starts from the opposite side. They meet each other beside the hut, as planned, and are delighted that the Wireless can be heard plainly. They hear the War in Europe has been over a few weeks, and as they wander back to their tent trying not to show a reaction, they can't help wondering how long it will be before it's over in the Far East too! The friends decide to repeat this walk at the same time the following week, to find out if anything is happening there too. We mustn't show any sign to the Guards that we're jubilant.

Time matters a lot now, as Christian is becoming more emaciated by the day, and the other two are concerned about his ability to last much longer. Each day, when working in the heat, James doubles up for Christian when no Guards are watching, allowing the latter a few minutes rest to recharge his batteries. Each day, though, it takes longer for him to recharge. Having now heard the world news, the three go to sleep with renewed hope of an early release. Christian's thoughts turn to Hannah tonight, and how she'd never recognize him now.

As Christian falls into a deep sleep, he has a strange dream in which he is lying by the edge of a road, and leaves are falling from an overhead tree. They keep falling till he's covered from head to foot in a matter of minutes. Not only do they cover his body, they suffocate him and it's this feeling of not being able to breathe that wakes him with a jolt! Christian realizes the dream is telling him something . . . . telling him that although he has feelings for the beautiful nurse Malay, which may possibly grow into love one day, that it is Hannah he really loves and wants to be with for the rest of his life. The realization is a bolt out of the blue, but the problem is, how is he ever going to tell Hannah of his change of heart, or Malay too, for that matter, while he's stuck in this godforsaken place!

The next morning, during work building the road, Christian suddenly keels over and falls into a muddy ditch. His two friends look on in dismay as they feel unable to help at that moment. There are two Guards very close by. One of the Guards comes over and prods Christian with his rifle butt to see if he's still alive, upon which Christian tries to get up but each time, falls back in the ditch again. This prompts the Guard to get his Superior, and as he does so, James and Stuart fear the worse! Without thinking of his own safey, James picks Christian up in his arms, and wedges him between the two of them, placing the spade under his arm to make it look like the latter is digging. When the Guard and his Superior see Christian standing and holding his spade, they walk off muttering something in Japanese, probably thinking he's wasting their time!

Christian has tears of gratitude in his eyes, and the three carry on till the day's end, working closely together, so it doesn't appear like they're propping up Christian as he struggles to reach the end of the shift.

The Guards never take their eyes off their prisoners, almost hoping the latter will do something wrong so they can administer some punishment. A sharp hit with a rifle butt gives the poor people enough fear to keep going, even if they're fatigued bodies want to collapse to the floor. This is what almost happened to Christian during the hottest part of the day, and an unbelievable thing occurred.

Hannah witnessed the whole episode as she crossed the compound on her way to the Commandant's buildings, even though the identity of any of the male prisoners cannot be seen by the female prisoners in the Camp that she's captive in. However, the fields everyone works in are not far away, and Hannah felt distressed this particular day on seeing a male prisoner apparently getting into trouble with one of the Guards. She feels so sorry for the poor man, not realizing for one minute that this man is Christian, the love of her life!

On this day also, the three friends arrive back at the Camp, to be met with much noise and commotion. The Japanese Commandant, looking flushed and agitated, is standing in the centre of the compound, signalling for all prisoners to muster in the compound for a meeting. There is a document in his hand, which obviously is the cause of the commotion. With the interpreter by his side, he announces, in a voice completely devoid of any emotion, that the War in the Far East, is now over, and as from today, they are all free to leave the Camp!

A huge cheer goes up from the prisoners, even the ones who are so exhausted that they previously hadn't enough energy to utter a word! Everywhere, there is chaos, and the whole Platoon are even unaware of the retreat of their Captors, who seem to vanish into thin air! The news takes a while to sink in, as the poor prisoners have harboured feelings of no hope, and negativity, for so long. No-one had expected to feel freedom for a long time yet.

The Platoon have only been prisoners for a few months, or at worst, less than a year, but because they've been out of touch with the rest of the world, and everyday life, it seems like an eternity. They gather together in a dazed fashion, trying to decide on the next move. The three friends walk back to their accommodation block, as at this moment, gathering their belongings is all they can think of, even though they have very little to actually pack. Christian has to find one more ounce of energy to be able to walk out of the Camp, their walk to freedom, the most important walk of their lives.

They almost stumble over each other in their rush to get out of their nightmare existence, the Camp, the compound, the area! The fact that they now have to face another nightmare, their survival, and walk to freedom, doesn't cross their minds, so elated are they all to be free at last. They set off down a footpath, putting one foot in front of another, heading in one direction, South to Bangkok.

Uncannily enough, Christian passes right beside the buildings housing his girlfriend, who hasn't yet been told the War is over! The women are about to be told though, and to be released to walk to freedom, down the exact same footpath that Christian and his Platoon are walking at this moment. There is not much conversation between the men, and not one of them, in their rush to leave, thought about grabbing any water or food remains from the Camp before they left.

James states that there should be jeeps travelling from North to South, maybe taking injured soldiers to and from Hospital, that could possible give some of them a lift, at least part of the way. The jungle terrain is unrelenting, making progress difficult. They can only manage a few meters at a time, before getting out a knife and cutting back the dense foliage. Luckily, one of the men had the sense to grab a knife before leaving, knowing they will need one. They're own knives were confiscated on arriving at the Camp along with any weapons. They have to stop regularly, as all the men are in need of nourishment, and desperately search for anything in the trees that may be edible. They will even consider an insect at this point, so starving are they!

The lack of water to drink if beginning to get to all the men, and they all hope to find a stream or pond along the way. It is this thought that keeps them moving forward.

A few hours more into their hike, and one of the Platoon suddenly collapses onto the footpath, presumable from fatigue, but a quick inspection by Lieutenant Foley confirms the latter's worst fears. It's Malaria. Tragically, there's nothing that anyone can do to help the sick soldier, as no-one knows where the nearest Hospital is located. As they've just come from being imprisoned, none of them has any painkillers or drugs of any sort on them. As Lieutenant Foley cradles the sick man in his arms, the others cannot help thinking that underneath the loud-mouthed, stern exterior, lies a sympathetic and caring person. What a good combination of characteristics, thinks Christian.

Just as the Lieutenant is telling the Platoon to go on without him, and he'd stay with the sick man, someone at the front of the Platoon suddenly shouts that there's a clearing not far ahead, and he can hear the sound of running water. The men run forward towards the welcome sound, and there, like a sparkling jewel cascading through some bushes, is a waterfall.

The Lieutenant then carries the sick soldier on his back, into the clearing where there's water, and lies him down under a tree. While the men take their fill of the cool, fresh water, a sip at a time, like they have been trained to do, another soldiers drops to the ground, apparently unconscious. As the Lieutenant rushes over to him, he then diagnoses another case of Malaria, as the man has such a high fever, it's easy to spot.

Christian and James notice there are homes with thatched leafy roofs, scattered around the edge of the clearing, almost hidden by trees. Suddenly, out of one of the houses steps a family, including four women and a group of children, curiously scanning the distraught group of men. As a few of the men walk towards the women, one of the latter steps forward and shouts to Christian,

"It's me, Malay, don't you remember me? I looked after you in Hospital, and when you left, you said you'd come back to me."

Christian rushes forward into her arms, and they embrace for a long time, to the amusement and curiosity of the rest of the men.

"Of course I remember you, how could I ever forget?" replies the tearful Christian, trying to control his emotions, but not doing a very good job.

Malay excitedly believes Christian has returned to her, and obviously doesn't know they came upon her village purely by accidident. How is he going go free himself of this predicament, thinks Christian. Since he's been in prison, his feelings have changed, and now all he wants is to get back home to America, and Hannah.

"I prayed you would come back to me, and have been waiting for you. I was sure one day you'd be released, and would immediately find a way to be with me." replied Hannah, lovingly and enthusiastically.

Due to language difficulties, the circumstances in Hospital at the time, and misunderstandings, it's easy to see how Hannah could have misconstrued Christian's intentions, when what he really meant, was that he would come to Burma after the War was over, on a visit, and look her up.

He tries an explanation, "Look Hannah, you know when I met you in Hospital, I became very fond of you, as you helped greatly in my recovery, but all the time, my intention has been to return to America, and my long-time girlfriend. I mistook your empathy and caring ways, when I was ill, for real love. I was confused, feverish, and felt very vulnerable at the time. When I said I'd come back to you, I meant I'd visit you again when I'm a free man one day. I knew I had to fly home to America first, to recover from the effects of War, and only after that, would I be able to travel back here to see you again.

Believe me, I'm so fond you, I know that much is true. It's not enough, though, to be with someone for a lifetime. My Platoon has been imprisoned in a Japanese Prisoner-of-War Camp for months, and there was no way I could contact you to tell you of my change of heart, or that I intend to go home to my girlfriend in America after our release. It's purely by chance we passed through your village, as it's on our walk South to freedom. We're on our way down to Bangkok eventually, after first collecting our belongings at the Camp. We all realise we're lucky to be alive, and to be released from that nightmare of a prison. Now the War's over, we must leave the country as soon as possible. I'll never forget you, your kindness, your love."

Christian embraces her and walks off, leaving a tearful Malay, who is being comforted by the rest of her family, who have been watching from the steps of their home. The rest of the Platoon, who've been resting and drinking water while the couple said their farewell, are now glad to be on their way, refreshed. In one way, Malay is relieved the men are still alive, and have survived the War and terrible conditions at the Camp, but in another way, she feels betrayed by the first real love of her life. She truly believed he was in love with her too, and thinks he really did give her the wrong messages when in Hospital. How wrong could I have been, she thinks, lesson learnt.

Christian is just about able to walk now, and despite being skeletal, the adrenaline released with the realization they're all free men now, enables him to keep moving forward. Malay knows she must get the motivation to get through everyday life once again, without looking forward to spending her life with the beloved Christian. Her job as a nurse at the Field Hospital, is obsolete, now that the War is over, and she hopes to be employed again as a nurse at a different Hospital elsewhere. She hopes emotional healing will begin soon, with her family to help.

In the meantime, the Platoon, including the three friends, struggle on down muddy paths, enduring yet again, the heat and humidity, occasionally tripping over jungle vines hanging from the trees, and all the time, suffering from extreme exhaustion. They were all able to drink water at Malay's village previously, but lack of food for so long, has made it's presence felt, with the small bodied men suffering more.

Suddenly, Christian collapses into the mud, and the other two rush to him. He's put onto James' back, who luckily has some vestiges of strength left, due to his immense size, no doubt! They don't want to stop anymore en route, in case they lose momentum.

As twilight takes over from the bright sunshine, a noise can be heard, a faint rumbling like thunder. As it gets nearer, the men realize it's a huge truck, and it's slowing down when the driver spots them. He tells them he's come to pick up any stranded prisoners from the North, from Prisoner-of-War Camps, and was ordered to do this by telephone, from the U.S Office of the Military.

A cheer goes up from the Platoon, which now numbers less at this point, due to having lost two comrades to illness en route the previous day. How tragic, thinks Christian, that we all had to bury them in the jungle, only twenty-four hours before they're all rescued. The men scramble into the back of the truck, mostly crying tears of joy, knowing now that they're definitely safe.

The driver tells them he will drop them off at their original Camp where they started the posting, and that it will take many hours to reach there, due to the bad state of the roads. The men, though, don't care, as they bounce around in the back of the dusty, dirty truck. They're all in need of nourishment, a wash and familiar surrounding. Many of them fall asleep, and some actually say a prayer of thanks, so grateful are they to be alive and returning to see their families again.

As the truck arrives at the Camp, the men disembark and go to their accommodation which is there just as they had left it, all those months ago. The Military had already organized someone to make them food for them, for when the Platoon arrived back. The meal of rice and beans that is waiting for them, never tasted so good!! The Platoon settles down for the night inside the tents they'd had previously, with a statement from Lieutenant Foley that they will be told the plan to evacuate Burma, the next morning.

As Christian falls asleep, he has a dream about a part of the fighting he'd rather forget. It was the Japanese man whom he'd had face to face combat with, during the worse part of the conflict. Their eyes had met, while they stood barely three feet apart and it was a case of who fires first. It was Christian who got in with the first shot, albeit he was frozen to the spot in shock. In his mind, in that split second, was the thought, it's either him or me!

From that moment, Christian's life was destined never to be the same again. He has never been able to forgive himself, or forget it, like it's imprinted on his brain forever! As he gets to the part where he's fired the fatal shot, he wakes, sweating and trembling. He can't wait till morning, when sleep is over and there's no chance of a repetition of that dream.

However, despite all attempts to get over this incident, it continued to plague Christian for the rest of his life.

CHAPTER EIGHT

THE WOMEN ARE FREE

Meanwhile, back in the women's workhouse-type Camp, news of the end of the War is about to be leaked through. There has been a delay, as the Commandant has not been there for a couple of days, and it's his job to make such an important announcement. As far as Hannah is concerned, with her temporary job behind her, she's now putting her search for Christian on hold, until her release from this prison without bars.

This situation is something she hadn't accounted for when making her original plans. Each day, she and the other women in her accommodation block, had performed their duties under extreme conditions of heat and lack of nourishment. Each day, she'd become more and more depressed, wondering what is going to happen to her in this dreadful place, this hell on earth.

On this particular day, she wakes with a strange feeling, in an environment she can't put her finger on. Even though she's in the same bunk in the hut, around her there's silence, when usually there's movement and noise. Today, she must have overslept, and Hannah is suddenly fearful as to what the outcome of this will be for her captors.

She needn't have worried though, as today is freedom day! Obviously, the other women had woken first, and gone outside, she thinks. So up Hannah gets and rushes to the door dragging on her trousers and top. The scene that meets her eyes is like something out of a movie set! The women are gathered in a circle around the perimeter of the compound, with the Japanese Commandant in the centre of the circle, with an interpreter standing by his side.

In the Commandant's hand is a large document which he is reading from, and there is silence from the women. Suddenly a cheer goes up and the women jump up and down on the spot, hugging and embracing each other. The words uttered by the unfeeling Japanese man are ones they hadn't expected to hear fo a long time. The War in the Far East is now over!!

After the initial shock and then cheering, the women feel a sense of disbelief, wanting someone else to tell them what to do next, it's like they. re robots that need to be operated by remote control! They have been institutionalised for the time they've been kept like prisoners. They all collect in groups to decide what to do next, with the first step uppermost, being just to get out of that prison!

Hannah is in a group of six women from her accommodation block that decide to start walking down the only path they know of, the one which leads South, past the Prisoner-of-War Camp where Christian spent the last few months. Without waiting to grab water or any items of food, the women take the only possessions that they were in when captured, which wasn't much, just the clothers they stood up in.

As they start walking, Hannah suddenly thinks about the necessities of life, which no-one had thought of . . . . food, and water. It seems like they're not priority at this moment in time. Energy to move is there to begin with, as adrenaline is released from the effects of shock. After struggling through the dense jungle for over an hour, the six decide to sit down in the shade for a rest. As they do so, one of the women says she can hear the sound of running water, a sound so inviting, that she gets up and starts running down the path. The others get up and follow, already tasting the refreshing water with their taste buds.

The sound gets louder, so they know they're on the right track. Two minutes later, and the waterfall is in sight between bushes in a clearing. After sipping on the clear, cool water for a while, Hannah looks up and is aware for the first time of houses surrounding the clearing, locals standing outside them, and looking on in amusement and curiosity.

Ironically, the village happens to be the home of nurse Malay. It's her family that rush out of their home to help the group of women. It's Malay that invites them all into their home, and shares food, and a cup of their locally-made tea, with the grateful women. The family sit in a circle on the floor, and the women copy them, well aware of how lucky they are to be welcomed into a stranger's home.

Two of the women are reluctant to eat though, and Malay recognizes the first signs of illness, possibly Malaria. One of these women is Hannah. The kindly nurse requests that the two sick women stay at her home while she takes care of them, while the others can complete their trek to freedom. The two sick women agree, realizing they don't have much choice anyway. After an hour of rest and food, the other four leave, with emotional farewells leaving the sick women exhausted. Hannah can't believe receiving such care and support from a complete stranger.

Aready, Malay has gone into nursing duties, providing drugs for the fever, which she has kept after leaving her job at the Hospital. She also prepares broth to help them regain their strength, ironically it's the same recipe that she gave Christian when he was ill, and helped him recover. Nurse Malay then puts both into some spare hammocks on the balcony to sleep.

In the morning, she checks on her patients, and finds their fevers are less, and they both had had a reasonable amount of sleep. Now is the time to ask them how they became to be captured, Malay speaks quietly,

"Where have you all been, to become weak and emaciated? Don't tell me you have been prisoners too? I didn't know the Japanese took women prisoners, only soldiers, and believe me, I've looked after many a wounded soldier, and nursed them back to health. I worked until the War ended, in a Hospital not far away, and saw terrible injuries and death. I'll never get over seeing those young men suffer like that, and struggle to find a purpose in it all."

Hannah feels it's time for her to speak, now she's feeling a little better. Quietly, she explains to the nurse,

"I came over here from America to work temporarily as a Teaching Assistant in a school outside Bangkok. When my eight week posting was over, I decided to search for my boyfriend, who is a soldier fighting with his Platoon, also from America. Then I heard from a local that there was a Camp full of American soldiers stationed near here, and during my search, I happened to walk in an area where the Japanese were patrolling. They captured me at gunpoint, and put me into this type of Prison Camp, and I was so frightened. Luckily, it was not for long, as the War Ended, but if it had gone on much longer, I'm sure many of the women in my accommodation would have got very ill, or would have died. The work, and heat, combined to render us weak and exhausted. We were prone to illness all the time."

Obviously by now, Malay has picked up the fact that Hannah and her boyfriend, are both American, and there is an inkling in her mind that they may be connected to her in some way, although in what way, she's not sure . . . . not yet! Hannah also is wondering about fate, and has it played a part in all this.

She puts two and two together, as there are so many pointers to the fact that this beautiful Burmese nurse, this caring kindly soul, could possibly be the same person that Christian told her about in his last letter?? How could Hannah possibly feel anything but a fondness, for this person who put herself out for the comfort and safety of the women prisoners.

The town's name is the same as the one on the postmark of Christian's letter, and the Camp, and the Hospital where he was taken, are all in the same area of Northern Burma. Added together, it all seems to point to the fact that this could be Nurse Malay.

Hannah tries hard to cover up any emotion that will give away the fact that she knows who Malay is, and starts suddenly to feel uncomfortable, being looked after like this, almost to the point of feeling guilty, yet she has no reason for this.

. She wants to leave the village soon, before Malay gives up any more information that she may not want to hear!! Malay, though, notices that Hannah is agitated, and puts it down to her illness, but when the latter admits she's now well enough to think about leaving, Malay asks her to stay a little longer, at least till the next day, to be sure both women have eaten proper food and have the strength. In fact, she says she knows of a local man, with a truck, who makes regular trips down South to the outskirts of Bangkok, on business, trying to sell his agricultural produce there in the markets.

After a little persuasion, Hannah and Bintang, the other Burmese woman, do say they'll stay till the next day, to accept a lift from the truck driver. Supper is served by the caring nurse, who seems to enjoy having people to care for. After all, it's her profession, and she's used to it. Malay takes this opportunity to ask more details of Hannah's life, and what it's like living in America, as opposed to Burma.

Hannah tells her only a little, to satisfy the nurse's curiosity, "Yes, it's very different living in America. First, the culture is hard to define, but women have more say in what they do with their lives, compared to here. Having said that, I havn't been here long enough to be an authority of Burmese life, but what I've seen is only the result of War, and it may be different in peacetime. I would love to return here one day, to see the beauty of this country when the world is not at War with each other."

The two women exchange a momentary glance, before Malay goes to prepare the supper, of rice and vegetables. They sit cross-legged, and by now, both of the sick women have recovered enough to want to eat solid food, thanks to the drugs the nurse provided, which Hannah is sure is Quinine, a well-known remedy for Malaria. They eat in silence, relaxing for the first time in ages. After supper, Malay disappears outside to find the truck driver, and ask him if he can take two women passengers the next day. The driver agrees, and says he's happy to help. He says he'll be calling for them at 9am the next morning.

Hannah is still wondering if she can leave the village before the nurse asks any personal questions, as up to now, she's not told the latter the name of her boyfriend. That will surely give the game away, she decides. Malay says she hopes the other four women prisoners who left the previous day, managed to get home, and Hannah assures her of this, as she knows they're agricultural workers, who were captured in fields not far from the Camp, and also that they've not far to walk to get to their homes. This is not the case with Bintang and herself though, who both need to get to Bangkok.

Hannah thinks it a good idea to change the subject of her own life, and tell Malay a little about what happened to her companion, Bintang.

"Bintang was captured by the Japanese, as she dared to answer back to a high ranking soldier, at the start of the War in the Far East. She was young, and leaving her school, when the soldiers marched through her village. When most villagers feared the worse, and hid in their homes, she dared to approach the leader of the group, asking what the Burmese people had done, for Japanese soldiers to be marching through like they're taking over the country!!

For her nerve, she was immediately taken as a prisoner, and marched with them to the workhouse in the North, where she performed laundry duties for the Japanese for many months. By the time I arrived there, she was working in the fields, as I had to do."

Malay tells the two women that they'll have their lift to Bangkok at 9am next morning, and it would be good for them to have a good night's sleep now. She is mesmerised by the tales of what happened to both women, and can only be thankful she trained as a nurse, to be exempt from being captured. The memories of what she saw in that Field Hospital, will be embedded in her mind for the rest of her life, she thinks.

In their hammocks that night, the two women are thankful to be alive, and cannot wait to see their families again. At 6am, they're woken by chickens belonging to the neighbours, who make their dawn chorus heard for miles around!! Malay checks on the women, to make sure they're well enough to travel, and gives them breakfast sitting on the floor, like Burmese always do. Hannah wants to go now, as every minute she's there, she's well aware that the dreaded question could be asked, "What is your boyfriend's name?" just out of curiosity.

Suddenly, there is a shout from outside in the clearing, from the truck driver, who says he's ready to depart in half an hour. Both Hannah and Bintang wash, and prepare to leave, thanking Malay for her amazing kindness to them. As the women embrace, Malay wishes Hannah good luck for her flight home to America, and at that moment, the latter is now positive Malay knows who she is. There is an exchanged glance, which tells Hannah that Malay knows, but it's also a glance which says, it's ok, and I wish you all the best for your future. As the two women climb into the back of the truck, trying hard to stop the flow of tears, Malay has the last word.

"Tell Christian I wish you both all the luck in the world."

Hannah waves, realising now that all is out in the open, Malay knows her identity, and notices the tears flowing down Malay's cheeks too. She feels such empathy for the other woman. Bintang's face is glowing with pride that she survived her ordeal in the Prison Camp, and is returning to her family on the outskirts of Bangkok. Her parents have been so worried about her, as she was barely seventeen years old when captured. She talks non-stop to Hannah, as the truck bumps down the crater-filled earthy road, the road to freedom.

In Hannah's mind, however, is plans for her return home, as up till now, she's been too busy with the process of surviving, to think any further ahead. First to work out is the arrival in Bangkok. She knows there are buses to the Airport from numerous places, as she's not sure yet where the truck will drop them off.

Hannah has a good idea, that is, to go to the Information Office for Tourists at Bangkok Airport, and find out what provisions there are for returning soldiers, prisoners or international workers—a type of Post-War evacuation process. She cannot believe the War is over after all this time, yet the news is received by her with mixed emotions, in a way. This is due to the fact that she now knows nothing about the demise of the love of her life!

The experience of her School posting is one she'll never forget. She'd become fond of her pupils at the School, and although sad that she only had eight weeks there, she's also glad to be leaving the country eventually. She cannot wait to get home to Amber, to see if her family has any news of Christian. It's the not-knowing, that is tearing at her heart strings all the time.

After another two hours in the back of the truck, the driver announces they're approaching Bangkok outskirts. Relief is written all over the faces of the two women. Bintang is almost home, as she comes from a village on the outskirts of the city, and says an emotional farewell to Hannah, wishing her luck for her future in America. Bintang walks slowly across the road, back to her family, her life, her loves, her home, at long last.

The driver requests from Hannah where she'd like to be taken, and she's surprised that he's prepared to take her to the Airport. She thanks him gratefully, and enters the building. Realizing she has no money to pay for a flight, Hannah knows she must call her parents with a reverse-charge call, and ask them to book a flight from their end, on behalf of her.

Up till now, they don't know what has happened to her since her departure from the School, so they must be really worried about her welfare, and beside themselves with anxiety.

The telephone booth is a welcome sight, and the voices at the other end of the phone are an even more welcome sound, with both parents crying into the mouthpiece! Of course they say they'll book her trip home immediately, all she has to do is wait in the Airport and call them again in a few hours. In fact, they had believed she had stayed on at the job in the School, as had heard nothing to make them think otherwise. If they'd known she was imprisoned by the Japanese, they would have been even more worried, as they have only known male soldiers being captured so far in the War.

It's an amazing feeling just being in a safe place, relaxing, and knowing she'll be home tomorrow. Hannah has so far omitted to ask her parents if they know of Christian's whereabouts, as she was hoping they would just come out with it straight away, if they did know something. Therefore, she's decided to wait till she rings them back about her ticket. Meantime, she just sits and thinks, imagining what it will be like to be in Christian's arms once again.

Two hours later, and Hannah is back at the telephon booth, asking her parents to pick her up when her flight arrives, and then the inevitable question . . . . have you or Christian's parents any idea what has happened to him, or his whereabouts?

Their reply does nothing to quell the rising anxiety in Hannah's mind. As she expected, it is completely negative, as no-one has any idea where he is as yet, only that the War has ended in the Far East, and prisoners have been released. Christian's parents expect to hear from him very soon, if he's able to get to a telephone, or even send a telegram. They say not to worry, but just to make sure she's alright and to get home, then all will be sorted.

Luckily, Hannah is booked on a flight which goes via Europe, then New York, and finally to New England, but the ticket needed to be rebooked, as her original booking was obsolete. Any obstacle now seems trivial after having experienced the trauma of War.

Lying on the departure building seats, she tries to sleep, but is too excited. She manages an hour early in the morning, but sleep is disturbed as she dreams of seeing Christian, not in a normal situation, but lying on the floor of a Prison Camp, with a Japanese soldier standing over him, pointing a gun to his head. An Airport announcement wakes her up from an otherwise upsetting dream. She can't help wondering if this dream is a premonition of what is to come, but hurriedly pushes it from her mind. She quickly realizes where she is, and prepares for the flight, trembling with excitement mixed with apprehension.

The long flight is spent in a state of drowsiness due to her lack of sleep, and the after-effects of having been ill so recently. As the plane flies low over New England to prepare for landing, Hannah is struck by the beauty of the colourful golden forests of the trees in the Fall, and she suddenly remembers the last thing Christian said to her before he left . . . .

"I will come back to you . . . . when the leaves start to fall."

CHAPTER NINE

PREPARATION FOR EVACUATION

Meanwhile, back in the Platoon's Camp in Southern Burma, it's time for the men to prepare for an evacuation. However, a few of the men are deemed to be not fit enough to travel to the Airport for their flight home. One of them is Christian. It seems hard for him to regain enough strength to be upright for more than a few minutes at a time. The plan is for Lieutenant Foley to remain at Camp with the four sick soldiers, for a few days, to give them chance to get stronger. The Lieutenant could have left, as the War is over, but he chose to stay of his own accord till the end . . . . like a ship's Captain who is the last to leave his sinking ship!!

The four men who are left, say an emotional farewell to their comrades, who are like brothers after fighting together. The men who are leaving, are going to be driven back to Bangkok in one of the old jeeps used to transport injured soldiers to and from Hospital, during the War. They are so malnourished, that to walk any further would be cruel, and they need to get home as soon as possible. They're not sick enough to stay with the others.

It has been difficult to get news to soldiers' families during the conflict, so every man just wants to see his own family again. There is a Military Doctor staying behind also, to organize the evacuation of injured and sick soldiers. The main problem with the four, is malnourishment, combined with after-effects of jungle sicknesses, nothing which a few days of food and rest won't cure.

In these few recovery days, Christian plans to write to Hannah, to let her know he's alive, and is being kept behind for a few days in a Camp for American soldiers, till he's well enough to make the flight home. He presumes Hannah is aware the War on the other side of the world, is over now. However, at this moment, there is only one supply vehicle to replenish medical supplies for injured soldiers, as mail is not considered necessary now that the conflict is over. So Christian writes just a brief letter telling her he'll be home very soon, and it doesn't even leave the Camp.

He starts the letter,

Dear Hannah,

I am at our original Camp here in Burma for a few more days, so will keep this letter brief. Due to malnourishment and weakness, myself and three other soldiers are recovering. There is a lot to tell you, and I know you will have heard that the War in the Far East is over. However, I've some explaining to do, and it will be better when we can meet again face to face. I've no idea how this letter will get to you, as supply vehicles are sparse, but I will find a way of mailing it.

I want to see you again to tell you of my circumstances at the time I wrote you the previous letter, then maybe you'll understand why it happened.

I'm on my way home in a few days, when strong enough to fly, so till then, when the leaves start to fall . . . .

Your beloved Christian.

Never mind, he thinks to himself as he snuggles into his bunk and tries to rest, Hannah will know he'll be home again, (even if she never receives this last letter), and she will understand what happened, for him to write the previous letter . . . . when the leaves start to fall.

Each day for a week, the four soldiers gain a little more strength, till by the end of the seven days, they're almost recovered. Lieutenant Foley has been a blessing to them all, with his emotional and physical support. Who would have thought, right at the beginning of the conflict, that this loud, stern American, could be a calm and supportive man in peacetime!

Christian thinks that this is what being at War does, it changes people, and it brings out the best in some, and the worse in others.

On the seventh day, the Lieutenant has ordered a jeep to be used to take the men, plus two walking-wounded, down to the Airport, to catch a Military plane back to America. They have put on weight, and are stronger in mind and body. However, two of the men, including Christian, are still traumatised mentally. They have regular nightmares of being in battles, being shot, and hurling grenades into bushes with the ultimate horrendous blasts. Christian wonders if they'll ever go!

All there is to go through now, is the drive back to the waiting aircraft. It's not far, and on the way, the men discuss the outcome of the War, and how they will never understand what has been achieved by this conflict, with the purpose of it all being the most difficult part to digest. Christian thinks of what it will be like to see Hannah again, and that he should be home in time for when the first leaves start to fall . . . .

Little does he know that she has just completed exactly the same trek as him and the Platoon, and the only difference is that he will be flying home in a Military aircraft.

Before the men leave the jeep, the Lieutenant speaks to them all.

"Well, my men, you've all done an excellent job here in this jungle, and I'm happy to see you have survived, despite being imprisoned. I want to wish you all good luck for the journey home, and don't worry about anything, as your flight is sorted, and I'm sure your families will be at the Airport to meet you on your arrival in the US. There are a few soldiers who are still in Hospital, but they'll be sent home in a separate aircraft in the near future.

I cannot tell you how delighted we all are, that the War is over. We can now return to normal lives, our families, our health, and our pre-War occupations. I know you'll have flash-backs of the fighting, but it's normal, and they should slowly become less frequent. It's called Post Traumatic Stress Disorder, and the other name is Shell Shock. If it become troublesome, then see your Doctor, and I'm sure there'll be a remedy for it, to help you get through it.

At the Airport buildings, Christian made a decision not to telephone his parents from Burma, but to wait till he arrives on American soil, to give him chance to get over the worse of his emotions. Two hours later, the men are on the aeroplane, bound for America, and home. No sooner has he sat down, than he's asleep. He dreams of Hannah, and sees her outstretched arms waiting for him at the end of what looks like a long tunnel, with a bright light at the end of it. She is standing in the middle of the light and beckoning to him to come to her. As she does, leaves are falling all around her, then she disappears from view . . . . just as the leaves start to fall . . . .

CHAPTER TEN

HANNAH IS BACK IN AMBER

It's time now for Hannah to leave the aircraft, and there, on the tarmac, are her parents, holding out their arms in greeting. She runs over to them, and after many hugs and tears, they walk into the Arrivals building, arms around each other, almost like it they let go for an instant, they will lose each other again!

The three get into the family car, and Pop drives them all home to Amber. "Look," remarks Hannah, as they pull up outside their home in the leafy avenue, "The leaves are about to fall, and how beautiful this place looks, after what I've witnessed on the other side of the world."

After a brief supper, when Hannah lets both parents know she doesn't feel like talking at this moment, she goes up to her bedroom, to unpack her few belongings. There are far fewer, she thinks, than the ones she left with, all those months ago. She sits on her bed for a few moments, gazing out of the window, and thinking that tomorrow, she'll ask the questions she's wanted to ask, but daren't up to now.

Hannah wakes next morning with renewed optimism about the prospect of hearing good news about Christian, and maybe of seeing him again. He may not even have received any of her letters to him, anyway. She wonders what he is feeling like right at this moment, is he is still alive, where he is, and if he's even thinking about her too. She thinks to herself, how shocked he'd be if he knew about her imprisonment, her eventual release, the hazardous walk through the jungle, her illness, and finally, and most bizarre, her time spent at the village with nurse Malay!! Surely, this latter will be the biggest shock of all!

Little does either Hannah, or Christian, know, that they were actually both imprisoned by the Japanese, only half a kilometre apart, in the same area of Northern Burma, and that they both walked the same footpath to freedom, within a weeks or so of each other! That they had both passed through the same village where Malay lived, and that they had both contracted Malaria. They also had both been nursed by her, albeit in different places and circumstances, and both had survived the disease.

The next thing on the list for today for Hannah, is to find out from Christian's parents if there has been any news from him, since she had received her last letter. They must know something, she thinks, as if anything adverse had happened to him, a soldier's parents are the first to know. She wants to have a quick breakfast, then get over to their home, as they don't even know she has arrived back from Burma.

Just as she is going out of the kitchen door, the Wireless gives out an annoucement about world news. She listens as it may tell her if there are any injured American soldiers being kept in Hospitals in the Far East, too ill to be sent home. She does hear there are soldiers in the major cities, and efforts are being made by Foreign Offices to get them home as soon as they're well enough to make the trip. Obviously, no names are mentioned, but it does say families can ring the Foreign Offices to find out details. That's it, thinks Hannah, if Christian's parents have not heard yet, she will ask them to ring those Offices.

Standing at the Pitsley front gate, Hannah has a sudden rush of adrenaline, at the thought of what she may be about to hear. After a knock on the door, both parents are there in the hallway, hugging the person that they always wished would marry their only son, one day!

In Hannah's hand, she has the last letter from Christian, in case she needs to refer to it. After all, it may be all she has in the future to remember him by! The three sit together at the kitchen table drinking coffee, the place they always used to sit to exchange news, except there is one person missing, Christian!

Gradually, Hannah relates what has happened to her since she saw them last . . . . the arrival in Burma, the school posting, her trip North to search for Christian after finishing the post, and her eventual capture by the Japanese. This latter news fills the parents with dismay and horror. What Hannah does not tell them, however, is what happened to her there at the expense of the Japanese Guard, and the letter Christian wrote telling her of his new love for his nurse. In fact, she tells them nothing at all about nurse Malay, or having had met her on the freedom trip South.

The parents sit open-mouthed at some of the bits of news. Now it's their turn to speak, but at this moment, they have no news of Christian, apart from one letter he wrote them when he first arrived, and another saying the Platoon were moving North to another Camp. However, they've not been informed of him having been killed in action. Consequently, they are optimistic that he survived the conflict, and expect to hear from him literally any day now. They believe he will telephone from a booth at an Airport, to let them know he's safe and well, until they hear to the contrary.

Sipping yet another cup of coffee, Hannah finds solace in talking with his parents, as if it brings Christian closer to her, in mind and body. An hour later, and she is walking home with a little more hope than she had had on the way there. As she nears the end of the tree-lined avenue close to her house, she thinks she hears a voice. She stops in her tracks, as the voice sounds familiar, and it's calling her name very quietly, like a whisper in the wind, then it's gone! She looks all round her, through the trees that line the avenue, but sees nothing. There's no-one there, either up the street, or down. It must be my imagination, she thinks to herself, fearfully, and wondering what else may happen that her vivid imagination may come up with, in the next few days!

She spends the rest of the day going through her belongings, reminiscing with her parents, listening to the Wireless, and trying to relax. She is also recovering from near-starvation, so finds each hour is spent feeling a little stronger, both mentally and physically.

Every time the telephone rings, she jumps. Every time the postman calls with a letter for their box at the bottom of the path, she jumps. Every time there is a world news announcement on the Wireless, she jumps.

Early the next morning, Hannah wakes with a strange feeling in the pit of her stomach. She cannot identify why she should be feeling like this. It's a blustery day, and as the wind whistles past the window, she hears someone whispering her name, very quietly! The voice is coming from outside the window, and it sounds exactly like the one she heard the previous day amongst the trees outside! As it stops, Hannah wants to go outside, as if something or someone is calling her to. She's busy putting on a sweatshirt and jeans, when her Mom's voice shouts from downstairs that breakfast is waiting. The smell of coffee entices her even further to hurry with the process of putting on her clothes. At that moment, something makes her gaze up at the window, and there, fluttering down on it's own, is one brown leaf.

Halfway down the window, it stops!! Suddenly, her heart misses a beat. She knows, without any doubt, that this is Christian telling her that he's alive . . . . well . . . . and he's coming home to her!

She runs downstairs and out of the front door, shouting to her Mom, "Mom, Christian is coming home, he's just told me, he's alive!!"

"Really, Hannah, how do you know," remarks her Mom, astounded.

Hannah shouts back, "I know, because he told me before he left that he would be home this year, when the leaves start to fall, and the first one has just fallen past my window."

She runs down the garden path, and looks down the road. There, in the distance, getting off a bus with a large rucksack on his back, is Christian, holding his outstretched arms in greeting. He runs towards her, shouting, "Didn't I tell you . . . . I will come home to you . . . . when the leaves start to fall."

CHAPTER ELEVEN

NURSING HOME IN AMBER 2010

Hannah Mary Smith is sitting, gazing out of the window of her room in the Nursing Home in Amber. She has a sad, half smile on her weathered, wise face, while she's reminiscing about her beloved Christian and their family life.

She speaks quietly but eloquently considering her great age, "So . . . . that's how my story ends, with my darling Christian's return from the War in Burma, as he had promised me he would. He was not the same person as the Christian that had left to join the War. He was a severely changed man for ever after the conflict. He jumped at the slightest noise, had recurrent nightmares most nights, and he would wake in a cold sweat and reach for an imaginary rifle!

He had told no-one in his Platoon, that he could not get over having killed a Japanese at point blank range, literally face to face . . . . until he came home after the War. He told me. He said how different it was from just firing a weapon indiscriminately, without ever seeing your enemies' face. You have to look into their eyes, while you take their life! He truly believed he would forever be haunted by the look on the man's face.

As time went by, his nightmares became less in frequency, his memories of the fighting faded a little, and we went on to have a family, a boy called Nicholas, and a girl, called Amy, whom we both adored. Life in Amber slowly returned to normal, and Christian got a part time job in the Military Office, dealing with peacetime pursuits. We were as happy as we could be in the circumstances, and were very much in love.

Christian wrote letters to nurse Malay in Burma, thinking he owed her at least to keep in touch, and let her know he was recovering from the effects of the War. He said he would never forget her kindness, and after I had related my experiences to him, of my escapade in Burma, so long ago, he agreed that we both owed her a debt of kindness. Consequently, we posted photographs of our children to her, and she also mailed us pictures of her new husband and family. We both wished each other happiness and luck for the future.

When I had told Christian about my school posting, my search for him, and my capture by the Japanese in Burma, he thought I had incredible courage. The ultimate irony was when we both found out that we were prisoners in two adjacent Camps, without ever knowing it! Many were the times that we discussed our imprisonment, comparing our treatment. However, I have never told Christian of the assault I experienced at the hands of that Japanese Guard, and will keep it a secret and take it to my grave.

Ten years ago today, my beloved Christian passed away. As he took his last breath, he asked God to forgive him for having killed that one man. He then stared straight into my eyes, and slipped quietly away . . . . just as the leaves started to fall . . . .